DIARY of a PET TURKEY

BASED ON A TRUE STORY

by Joanne F. Ingis

drawings by Binny

🍎 BLUE APPLE BOOKS

I dedicate this book to my wonderful parents,
and to Paul, Benjamin, and Stephen.

-J.F.I.

Text copyright © 2011 by Joanne F. Ingis
Illustrations copyright © 2011 by Binny
All rights reserved / CIP data is available.
Published in the United States 2011 by
🍎 Blue Apple Books, 515 Valley Street, Maplewood, NJ 07040
www.blueapplebooks.com
First Edition 9/11 Printed in China
ISBN: 978-1-60905-091-7

2 4 6 8 10 9 7 5 3 1

NOTE:

Turkeys are wild animals.
It is not a good idea to approach a turkey.
They can bite, snap, and peck at you.

I'm the only turkey in my family.

Here I am when I was just an egg.

HOW TO SET UP AN INCUBATOR
FOR A TURKEY EGG

- Place the egg gently in the incubator. It should be turned three to five times a day at regular intervals. You may want to mark the egg with a soft lead pencil so that you are turning it exactly 180 degrees each time.

- The water reservoir in the incubator should be kept full. In addition, the egg should be misted each time it is turned with fresh, room-temperature water.

- Before the egg hatches, you may hear peeping sounds coming from it, and the egg may roll on its own! On the 25th day, stop turning the egg. This is so the turkey can get into hatching position. The egg usually hatches on the 28th day. The egg will hatch. The hatching process for turkeys can take up to ten hours. Do not help the turkey hatch.

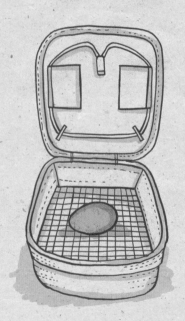

Incubator must be kept between **99–100 degrees** Fahrenheit.

All eyes are on me while I hatch.

Everyone watches and waits.

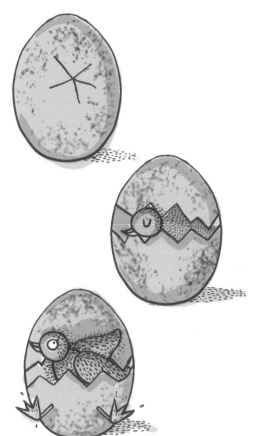

It takes me a while to push my feet out of my speckled shell.

I stay in an incubator for one whole day.
Then I am put in a small box.

The family keeps my tiny "room" warm.
It is cozy in here.

One morning when I am
peeping, Dad says,
"Our pet sounds different."

TURKEY SOUNDS

- A wild turkey makes at least 28 different sounds, or calls, and each has a meaning—from calling a mate to keeping the flock together.

- Besides the gobble, a turkey can also cackle, yelp, hoot, or purr.

- Males—or toms—gobble.

- Females—or hens—do not gobble. They make a clicking or clucking sound.

- A fully-grown adult can sound like a barking dog.

He thinks I sound
like a squeaky marker,
so he names me "MAGIC MARKER."

When I was little, most of my feathers were light brown. There are still some that are light. Others are darker brown, and some are white.

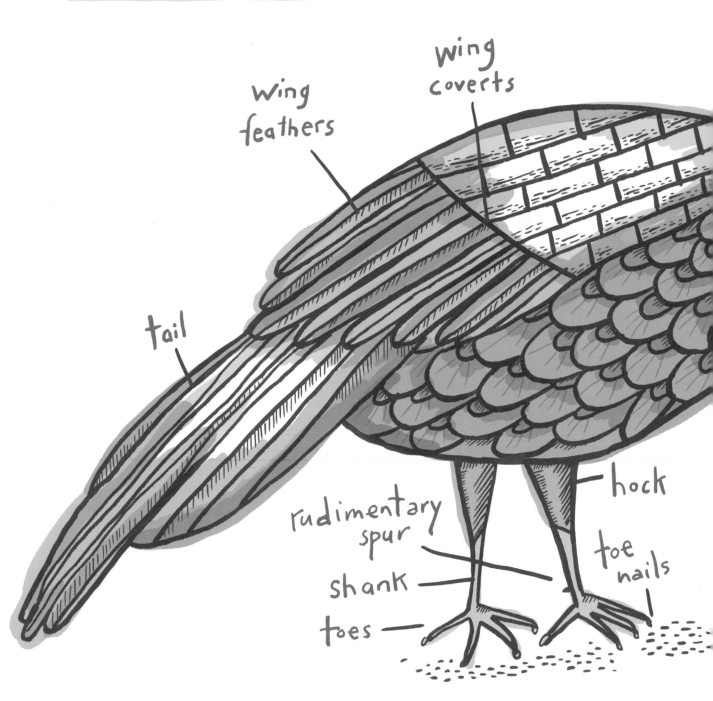

wing feathers

wing coverts

tail

rudimentary spur

shank

toes

hock

toe nails

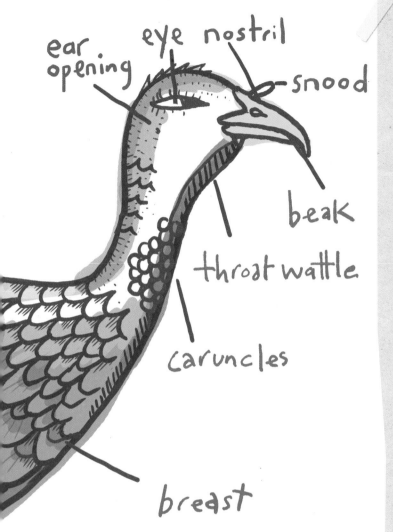

ear opening

eye

nostril

snood

beak

throat wattle

caruncles

breast

The feathers on my back glisten in the sunlight. They are red, blue, green, and even a little bit purple. Everyone says how pretty I look.

Until I am six months old,
I live indoors.

I stay in a brooder in the living room.

I hear someone say, "This room stinks!
Magic Marker is smelling up the house."

So they move me and
the brooder to the garage.

WHERE DO TURKEYS LIVE?

- Once the male and female turkeys have mated, the hen makes a nest.

- A hen's nest can be made in a shallow dirt depression in the ground that is hidden by grass.

- Wild turkeys live in areas that have both grasses and trees.

- Grasses provide a food source for the adult and poult.

- Trees give the turkeys a place to roost and rest and also provide a source of food.

When I get too big
for the brooder, Dad builds
a pen in the backyard.

He makes a "room" for me
with a chicken wire fence.

My place is under the steps
that lead to the kitchen.

When I was little, I ate small pellets of food.

The pellets I eat now are bigger, like me.

TURKEY DIET

Wild turkeys forage for food:

- acorns
- seeds
- wild berries
- roots
- tubers
- leaves
- small insects (including beetles and grasshoppers)

Tasty!

Now that I am older, I also eat bugs, worms, and bread.

One day while I am sitting on Mom's lap, a fly lands on her shirt. I eat it. Delicious!

Sometimes I pull at Mom's hair with my beak.

She thinks I'm grooming her, but I think
her soft hair would make a good nest.

Everyone smiles when I peck at Grandma Anne's toes.

Everyone except Grandma!

Peck Peck!

Grandma makes a shooing motion.

It looks like she's about to take off and fly.

The kids laugh.

I can fly, but not too far.

One day I fly high up to the top
of the neighbor's roof.

I walk down the roof slowly and make my way back to the ground.

Yipes

CAN TURKEYS FLY?

- Wild turkeys can fly for short distances, sometimes at up to 55 miles per hour.

- They can run 25 m.p.h.

- They can glide for a mile without flapping their wings.

- Domesticated turkeys cannot fly—they're too heavy.

me and Baby Isaiah

I like to play with
Baby Isaiah.
He is just my size.
I can put my wing
around him.

Julie is our neighbor.
She likes to
play with me and
give me hugs.

me and Julie

HOW BIG ARE WILD TURKEYS?

BABY TURKEY
weight at birth:
less than one pound

ADULT FEMALE
weight:
8-10 pounds

ADULT MALE
weight:
16-24 pounds

5-YEAR-OLD CHILD
weight:
35-40 pounds

Here I am at 10 months old.

Something is not right.

I am inside, hanging out under the table.

Mom wonders whether I am hurt.

She asks several times what

I am doing under there.

Only I know.

I am trying to lay an egg!

Finally, it happens—right there in the kitchen.

MY grandchild!

Mom is thrilled. She cradles the egg and calls it her "grandchild."

Mom knows my egg will not hatch because it was not fertilized by a tom.

Oooh!

TURKEY MATING

- In order to hatch, an egg needs to be fertilized by a tom.

- Wild turkeys mate in the early spring.

- In order to attract a mate, the tom gobbles loudly.

She also knows I do not have a good place to build a nest and keep my egg warm.

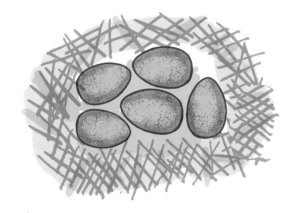

Mom shows my egg to everyone on the block.
Then Grandma cooks it for breakfast.
I hear Dad say, "This egg tastes just like
a chicken's egg!"

From January through April I lay 68 eggs—
Mom keeps a chart on the refrigerator.

Then I stop.
Mom is not happy.
I hear her say,
"Maybe next year
there will be
more eggs."

My family is waiting for a new supply of turkey eggs.

I will try not to keep them waiting too long.

MORE TURKEY FACTS

TOMS vs. HENS

- **MALE TURKEY:** a tom or gobbler

- **FEMALE TURKEY:** a hen

Toms are larger than hens. Their legs are longer; their heads and wattles are larger. The tom's snood is longer and hangs down the side of its face.

Toms grow beards (long black feathers that can be up to 9 inches in length) in the middle of their chests. The spurs on the back legs of the male grow two inches. The spurs on the back of the hen's legs usually do not grow.

TURKEY FEATHER FACTS

- Adult turkeys have between 5,000–6,000 feathers.

- The feathers keep the turkey warm and dry, allow him to fly, and attract the hen.

- There are no feathers on the head and upper part of the neck.

- The male turkey has more colorful feathers than the female.

- The hen is brownish in color. This coloring makes it easier for the hen to camouflage with the surroundings and protect her nest.